West of the Moon

MICHELE SPINA

West of the Moon

Translated from the Italian by
ANN COLCORD

Illustrated with etchings by
JAMES ABBOTT McNEILL
WHISTLER

PETER OWEN · *London & Chester Springs*

PETER OWEN PUBLISHERS
73 Kenway Road London SW5 0RE
Peter Owen books are distributed in the USA by
Dufour Editions Inc. Chester Springs PA 19425–0449

First published in Sicily by Sellerio editore © 1991
First published in Great Britain 1994
© Emma Spina 1994
English translation © Ann Colcord 1994
Illustrations © British Museum

A catalogue record for this book is available from
the British Library

ISBN 0–7206–0918–6

Printed in Great Britain by
St Edmundsbury Press Bury St Edmunds Suffolk

The Whistler etchings are
taken from the first Venice set of 1880
and the second set of 1886. They are
reproduced by courtesy of the Department
of Prints and Drawings of the British Museum.

Nocturne: palaces

1

He heard the sound of the train coming closer and then moving farther away in his mind. Why was he going to Venice? Recently he had been deciding casually to do now one thing and then another. His attempts came to nothing, or rather started from nothing and moved towards some vague, unfixed objective, chiefly because it was other or simply elsewhere. Venice was elsewhere.

But, he objected to himself, no one goes to Venice in the winter. He immediately realized, however, that this objection, this kind of thinking habitual with him, was the centre from which he set off, seeking to be elsewhere. Perhaps, he thought, we say men have the use of reason, while we ought to say that they have the use of thought, that is, a lesser sort of reason; they think from acquired knowledge, using grammar, in other words, and not logic. Or we could say, that whatever sort of reason is in general use, it is always of an inferior sort, full of idiomatic statements, of phrases like: The cat pisses on the mat. It was this vacant centre from which he intended to set off for Venice. He found himself enclosed in a sort of vague horizon, foggy, dreary grey, from which he saw Venice as a long strip of blue water and pink sky: an opening, if not exactly a way out. However, as the notion of Venice showed, aside from his own thought processes, undeniably a certain intellectual activity was going on in him, which could not be reduced to grammar. The most oppressive aspect of this kind of activity was its underlying uncertainty, haphazard distraction – a questioning, doubting, of any statement.

But why speak of statements? His thought rarely took verbal form. Sometimes the words that came to him were no more than a caption for an unexpected image. For example, a horse's head with the caption: Is it really like this or is it quite different? In the general uncertainty, one fact he was sure of was: That horse's head was not his own, did not come from him, nor belong to him; therefore the horse was the other, he deduced, and came from the infernal regions or some trick of lighting. But wherever it might have come from, heaven or hell, it had after all been granted him as a life companion.

'No,' he declared, all but jumping to his feet to give greater force to his affirmation, 'in this situation, grammar is better, and thinking is better.'

'What do you mean?' asked the woman seated across from him.

He excused himself: 'I am sorry,' he said, 'but I am convinced that even if one cannot employ logic one must at least stick with grammar.'

The other passenger gave him a look of concern and then nodded her head several times, judiciously. But who asked her? he said to himself. She had been the one to speak first.

She was a beautiful woman of a certain age, with large eyes, a long face and delicate features: one of the most conventional types of beauty, in other words. But her face was so pale it was almost unattractive. He thought, Perhaps if her hair were darker, or her eyes a darker, deeper blue, one could say with certainty: She is beautiful, despite her pallor.

'I was looking at you so intently because your beauty reveals itself little by little,' he explained.

'Oh!' she exclaimed.

'I mean, *signora*,' he continued, partly out of irritation and partly out of shyness, 'that at first sight, women of your age appear more elegant than beautiful. True beauty requires study. . . .' He stopped, shaking his head, obviously dissatisfied. 'Forgive me. I must have put my foot in it again.'

She laughed: 'Oh no!' she said. 'Don't worry, I beg you!'

He tried to smile. 'It always happens when I try to pay a compliment,' he said.

'Are you shy?' the woman asked.

'Not really. I am preoccupied with grammar. Some formulation, some example of grammar keeps on running through my head at the most inopportune times. On the other hand, grammar is a salvation. How could one find a way out of confusion without grammar?'

She nodded. She entirely approved of the idea of salvation by means of grammar, she said. What's more, she found grammar rather amusing.

11

So they continued to talk of many things, affably.

'Do you teach grammar?' she asked.

He shook his head: he was not a specialist in grammar, he said. He was in the timber business; or rather, he had been until two years before, when he found himself with a modest fortune and no family and had decided to stop dealing in timber and to travel.

She said she too had led a stationary existence until her mother died. . . .

That was not really what he meant, he explained. He could not call the life he had led stationary. His company had a branch in Hull, a rather sad city, full of seagulls, of large crows and other birds of prey; but he often travelled to Norway from there, and Germany, and also to Holland.

'Seagulls?' she asked. 'Don't you like them? You will certainly see seagulls in Venice.'

He reassured her: the Venetian seagulls were a refined variety. And then, he added, he didn't mean that he didn't like the city of Hull: it was merely run down, shapeless, that's all. The English countryside in any case was beautiful, very beautiful everywhere, even those elusive places: a land with clouds and fog in flight. 'But how beautiful!' he concluded. 'My God, how beautiful!'

She gave him a sympathetic look, nodding in the way that was now familiar to him.

'When I say beauty,' he explained, encouraged, 'I might mean disturbing, but also peaceful. That is the contradiction: it is like struggling to reach the conviction that it is best to succumb to vagueness. Beauty, you see, is never precise . . . moreover, it is fleeting. The question is: What next? *Quid tum?* So one moves towards what comes next, always with great uncertainty, actually with anxiety, only because, one must admit, nothing looks better to one now: so one puts off the moment of choice. The beauty of a woman also carries with it an invitation to temporize.'

'Is this what you meant, perhaps,' she asked, leaning slightly forward as if to confide in him, 'when you referred to my advanced age?'

'What?' he protested. 'You could be my granddaughter, although you must be at least fifteen!'

'How extraordinary!' She laughed, settling back against the seat. 'I see you as a grandfather. How old are you? Ninety-six? Ninety-seven? I'll be forty in February.'

'Very well,' he admitted. 'Perhaps not a grandfather.'

'Father?' she asked. 'My father was sixty-five when he died, and I was then nine.'

'Let's forget about the family,' he said. 'But sometimes there is a sense of kinship one cannot explain. No? Incredible! you will say. I agree: one cannot put one's faith in feelings that have no foundation. A single man like me, on the other hand, often lets himself be swamped by his feelings. I am thinking of Venice and Pushkin when I say this.'

'Why Pushkin?' she asked.

'Somewhere,' he explained, 'Pushkin wrote: "On the desolate tidal shore he stood, full of great thoughts." And then he mistakes fireflies for lanterns. It is not a matter of greatness of thought, but of the swollen roundness of waves constantly beating, doomed by inertia; the inert weight of water is a great force, as is the weight of sentiment in an empty soul like mine.'

13

They were silent for a while.

The train crossed a long bare stretch with grey trees, and made a whistling sound like wind rustling through trees, so it seemed to be flying low and silently, almost furtively, towards the shelter of the woods.

'What are these woods?' she asked.

He thought a while. 'Hazel-nut, locust. Without value, in any case,' he said. 'A coppice. Firewood: in other words, bundles of sticks.'

'Oh, what a shame!' she said, disappointed. She settled herself on the carriage seat. 'The advantage of first class is that often the compartments are empty. One can be peaceful and not disturbed by other people's chatter.'

'I am sorry,' he said. 'I didn't mean to disturb you.'

'On the contrary,' she said quickly. 'I was speaking of the two of us. For example, now we are speaking confidentially, to please ourselves, that is. But imagine being able to talk as we have talked in a crowded carriage?'

'You're right!'

'And then,' she continued, 'I rarely manage to talk. I really would like to, but men intimidate me and women bore me. Why do we feel a sudden impulse to say hello to someone? What is it that drives us irresistibly to speak? Sometimes I meet someone and cannot stop myself telling that person at once all the most private facts of my life, in imagination, in intention; but actually, I remain silent, with my lips sealed and a blank, fish-like expression on my face, as my mother used to say. But if I am going to Venice now it is also to go and talk to my dog. I also have a friend: my old piano teacher, where my dog spends half its time.'

'I find it much easier to talk with sheep,' he said. 'They are patient, good. They listen, even if they are a bit absent-minded. Dogs, as I see it, are too volatile: they interrupt, they are always changing the subject. In this respect, cats are better.'

'Wonderful!' she said. 'And where do you encounter sheep? I never run into any.'

'Certainly not in Venice,' he admitted. 'But the English countryside is full of them. There is a place northwest of Leeds where a friend of mine has a large house surrounded by land, almost what we would call a *tenuta*. It is near Skipton, a minuscule village: a place in the hills, a few trees here and there, a fine river and an indescribable landscape, damp and also windy. Very well. I used to spend weekends with her. Sometimes entire weeks. Not so much with my friend, however, as with her mother.'

'Wonderful!' she said again.

'Well, certainly it is a bit complicated,' he admitted. 'I became the friend of my friend's mother when she was about to bid me goodbye. I liked the place and used to go there whenever the younger woman was away. But to go back to the sheep, I remember one in particular. It wanted to jump over a wall on which I had been sitting, but every time it tried, it landed on its belly on top of the wall and was bucking back towards the place it had left.

'Tell me, beast, what do you find interesting there? I asked it. And so the conversation began, one thing leading to another. I began to tell it about my life, saying, for example, that two apparently contradictory tendencies were combined in me: one, an intermittent aspiration towards disinterested love, pure passion, and the other, more serious, towards comfort, or rather ease, if not actual luxury – a solid house like the one in which I had been a weekend guest, for example. That is, whatever romantic notions may pass through my head, I said to the sheep, I constantly desire the orderly existence of a village or a small rural community, quiet restaurants and polite waiters. What's more, I explained to the sheep, I think that once tranquil well-being is assured, love somehow follows and one can then, if one wishes, interpret that as romantic passion.'

'And the sheep?' she asked.

'The sheep didn't seem convinced,' he admitted. 'It continued to look over the wall towards the horizon, that vague line of hills and shifting mist, as if it were a specific destination: a point to be arrived at – the promised land in fact, and little by little, without paying attention to what I was saying, it tried a bucking jump towards the place of its sheepish desire. So that in the end, moved by pity for such constancy, I gave it a shove with both hands. It tumbled over the wall, which was rather high at that point and bordered a steep slope or ravine, and rolled down the slope for several dozen metres before it managed to scramble to its feet.'

'Poor beast!' she interrupted. 'Was it hurt?'

'I don't think so,' he answered. 'No, it climbed up the steep slope again rather quickly and started to bleat, asking me to help it get over the wall again. Inconstant beast! But you know how certain sheep are: *jocus et petulantia*. So

16

once I had managed, not without a certain effort, to pull it back into the field it had started from, its behaviour became less petulant and at the same time more familiar. Its attentions to me, if one could call them that, seemed more disinterested. That sometimes happens in a family in which everyone has his own concerns, but at the same time keeps an eye on the others. That's what the beast did, keeping its eye on me while grazing. To tell the truth, the eyes of these beasts, set as they are on the sides of their heads, have a focus so wide that they can take in at a glance not only the object of their attention, but also a great stretch of landscape. Anyone within that gaze has the impression of being one thing among many things, part of a mixture so diverse that any judgement becomes impossible: in other words, one doesn't see anything in oneself to be proud of or ashamed of any more, and this mitigates the bad and lightens the weight of the good, so that one feels freed from moral anxiety. The gaze of the beast also seemed affectionate to me, and even somehow understanding (for how rare it is for there to be understanding without affection). What's more, I talked about my life, and much of the time discoursed generally on love, on forage, and other topics that in a certain sense pertained to the sheep as well as to me.'

'And these trees?' she asked, pointing out the window.

'Yes, those are poplars,' he explained. 'A very good investment.'

'I have never succeeded in having such complicated discussions with my dog,' she said. 'Whatever tone I use when I turn to him, he invariably proposes that I toss him something to fetch.'

'If I mentioned discourse, perhaps it is best not to take me literally,' he admitted. 'I meant that some beasts somehow seem to companion our thoughts and in consequence seem also to influence those thoughts. I must admit that one thinks differently in the presence of sheep than in the presence of the Mayor of Venice. At least, that is my conviction. I reached it through a story that is too long and boring to be told to a beautiful woman.'

'Oh, no,' she protested. 'I'm very interested!'

'As you wish,' he replied. 'To be brief, at a certain point I realized I was thinking at random, or rather I began to think without urgency or aim, starting from any word at all. Every word in the dictionary has a primary meaning and I began in general to think of the first in a list of possible meanings, then to arrive usually very far away from it. Thought is also made for covering great distances. At the beginning I took this for granted. But then why choose that starting point? Why begin with that word? For example, why, in the middle of night, did I sit straight up in bed, brought suddenly awake, without warning, by the word "slide"? As time went by, I realized that it was not only words that could surprise me when they came, but also images: a horse, for example. This seemed more serious to me at first, because what meaning could a horse have? What could be the significance of such an image, in a moral sense, let's say, or even a logical one? What importance can a horse have, the image of a horse, I mean, perhaps captioned "Twelfth Night"? No! The truth is that we find ourselves always in the presence of the whole, and this is not an abstraction or a special mathematical quantity, variable with the circumstances or, as one says, the field. For me, don't you see, the concept of the whole is undoubtedly subtle, and too sophisticated to relate effectively to immediate experience. As a simple man, I see the whole as being exactly like everything outside myself; that is, the visible and invisible, literature, geography, carpentry, Latin, equitation or equitology: everything so far as it is other than myself is a metaphor, or even a metonym for everything else and therefore is also recognizable, that is, unforgettable. How could I forget what is other, if I have nothing other to think about? So the point of departure in the sense of the right, that is, the legitimacy, of thought, is precisely in this whole, or in everything other.'

After a pause, he said hesitantly: 'Perhaps I shouldn't talk to you about things like this. You might take it amiss . . . it might even distress you.'

'Oh, no, no! Do go on. Are you talking about the universe of the infinite or that of the horse?'

He smiled. 'Well, a bit of both. The advantage of this way of thinking, which is perhaps a bit incoherent, is its ease and clarity. Firmness, I ought to say. What could be more definitive than a horse's head with the caption "Twelfth Night", if it is assumed to be a metaphor for everything? There's no going beyond that. No question or doubt, however cleverly framed, could confound this figure. Freed from doubt, moreover, every interpretation can go as far as it pleases, can float freely, so to speak. The only possible variation in this state of things is when one's thinking is affected by variations in mood. One could be sad, even desperate, or contented or simply happy. . . .'

'And the sheep?' she asked.

'That's the point!' he exclaimed. 'The sheep too, or at least that sheep, thought randomly, I believe, that is, incoherently about everything. And yet: *jocus et petulantia*, I said of it; that is, unlike me, it did it, if not contentedly, at least somewhat happily, joyfully; and in this sense I believe wanted to give me a suggestion by example. Certainly, you may say, one could find similar leads even in Nietzsche, if one wished; but coming from the sheep they seem less lofty, and therefore evident and more persuasive.'

'Do you think the sheep and Nietzsche would agree?'

'This I don't know,' he said. 'However, even wanting to be pedantic, in this case, I think one could risk saying they shared the same line of thought.'

'I don't even manage to speak about Pirandello with my dog,' she said. 'I think he likes trees.'

'Well, you could also say this about my dog,' he said, 'if you assume that pissing against a tree is an expression of pleasure.'

'Do you have a dog?'

'A grammatical dog: the dog in one of those examples of grammar I was telling you about,' he explained.

The train sped silently through piles of fallen leaves in a wood of mature poplars.

She continued, pointing to the trees, 'Perhaps there were once elms here: the famous combination of vine and elm, the Veneto "planting", they used to call it. That would have been better than these poplar trees, which are all alike.'

'Hmmm!' he murmured. 'Unreliable wood, elm.'

'What are you saying?' she exclaimed impatiently. 'Don't you ever see trees? Only timber?'

'Professional hang-up!' he excused himself.

After an interval of silence, she began to speak, almost absent-mindedly: 'Did you marry your friend with the beautiful house in the country? Did you want to marry her for her beautiful house?'

'For her house,' he replied, 'and also partly for her money, but as I told you, she turned me down. Her mother, on the other hand, thought I would make a very good husband, serious and prudent; so she encouraged me to hope her daughter would change her mind. In other words, officially the mother and I both hoped for a change of heart on the part of the daughter, so I was authorized to visit the house. What furniture they had! Such skilful craftsmanship two centuries ago. Fortunately it was in a perfect state of preservation.'

She interrupted him, 'In other words, you don't bother to conceal your venal motives.'

'What's wrong with that? Marriage can be a very good business as well as very bad. Or at least in my day it could be. Does this offend you?'

'Forgive me,' she said. 'I was just talking, randomly, like your sheep. Do you believe me?'

'Of course!' he reassured her. 'What's more you are right. Even if the furniture was truly beautiful, I realized my motives were mixed. I was young then. . . . Nevertheless, I am pleased you now know something more about me.'

'I know nothing,' she protested, 'except that you love beautiful furniture and sheep and at the same time detest dogs that do nothing but piss against trees, as you say.'

They both laughed.

'You aren't always free-wheeling when you think,' she said after a while, secretly stealing a glance at him that was a mixture of curiosity and suspicion.

'I said free-floating,' he corrected. 'But one expression is as good as another. I clutch at grammar in my search for salvation from the lure of irreducible diversity. What I want is that the sheep seems to confront with a glance the difference between itself and the surrounding world, without anxiety, actually finding it all amusing. We on the other hand pretend there is a likeness, a family resemblance and possessions shared between one of us and the other; we become sentimental in the presence of the other.'

'Doesn't the sheep!' she said.

For a moment he looked at her, undecided: 'The closeness!' he finally said. 'For us proximity counts – not just a fortuitous proximity like ours in this train, but also the closeness now between me, for example, and that man of whom I spoke, who wanted to marry so he could have beautiful furniture.'

'That was the same man who was telling the story,' she interrupted. 'The story at least was told in the first person.'

'I don't know,' he said, shaking his head. 'It is so far away. Undoubtedly there is a nearness that endures long absences, and another nearness that distance dilutes and cancels. But we are only talking about various grades of nearness that we express with analogies and similes; metaphors, which are usually only metonyms, uncertain and dubious figures.'

'And the sheep,' she said. 'Forgive me if I keep bringing it up, but has it suggested a way out of doubt?'

'So I thought.' He laughed. 'But that isn't to say that the sheep's advice should be or even could be followed. Any beast, if consulted, seems to come out with the truth like an oracle. My sheep didn't actually speak, but through its behaviour I understood what seemed to me true, and its reply seemed mysteriously that of an oracle, that is, to be taken literally. The truth (as Aristotle himself said or implied) resides only in language, never in things, and yet language seems to be everywhere the truth appears to be, and even everywhere we search for illumination, including in sheep.'

'How important this sheep of yours is!' she commented, shaking her head.

'Well!' he said irritably, 'Important in a certain sense. . . . The Mayor of Venice would certainly never receive it and I have heard he receives. . . .'

'No.' She interrupted, reaching out to him. 'Please don't misunderstand me. I am almost overwhelmed by these animals of yours that offer solemn judgements, that speak the truth and offer good advice, even if later we fail to follow it. But I am not entirely stupid. Something of this solemnity also affects me. But could anyone say what I am saying, without conceding it's all in fun? That is . . . saying what I say to you, I am convinced and serious, but I also realize that you might think I was amusing myself at the expense of your sheep.'

23

He started to laugh, clearly placated. 'I am flattered when you laugh and also when you are serious. I wanted to amuse you.'

They were silent for a short time. Then she began once again to speak about her dog, explaining that it was a setter, perhaps a mongrel and therefore not at all valuable. It was a great big male dog measuring a full metre forty from the tip of its nose to the end of its tail.

While he listened to her, he realized with astonishment that the term for the pissing dog or cat had vanished from his mind, and he felt he had lost something, a motif or theme that, obsessive as it might be, was by now part of the furnishing of his mind. Who knows what will now fill that mental hole? he asked himself, worried, and to remedy his loss he tried to recover the word for the pissing of some other animal. Let's try to change the subject! he said to himself. It's a cow that is to piss.

He had never seen such a thing, but since, after all, it was merely a matter of constructing a simple phrase, he went on repeating: cow – subject, piss – predicate, in the field – locative complement. Everything in order, nothing seemed more realistic and less imaginary than a peaceful cow pissing. But, in spite of his efforts to keep it firmly within its grammatical boundaries, the phrase was not sufficiently well grounded and leaked out on all sides towards images that were visibly changing and even contradictory. He continued, for example, to see the field, the grass already a bit pale with frost on an autumn afternoon, smoking from the cow's piss, while the cow-subject had already gone beyond the horizon, lost, nowhere to be

24

found. In no case could one call this a finished proposition. It was, rather, a visual fantasy, open to amendment: one could put an elm at the edge of the field, and either some low shrub, or even a pine tree, not to mention the sky, which sometimes he could imagine as clear, other times as steamed over by low clouds. No, the phrase was no longer an entity with a single voice, or in other words, no longer had the reassuring precision it had once had.

For a start, this woman he had just met had erased an entire mental structure almost with a gesture. But, as if it were nothing, she continued to talk and talk. Water gushes with a beautiful sound! he thought, but then corrected himself: perhaps it is better to say flows. Gushing suggests flushing!

Salute, dawn

2

The room was cold, in spite of a huge heater which was boiling hot. 'Shall we light the fire for you, *signore*?' they had asked him. 'It takes some time to warm up because the walls are so thick.' Yet in the past two days he had felt the cold was increasing, in spite of the blazing fire; but it was a magical cold, bewitching rather than physical.

It was a large room, with a jumble of nineteenth-century furniture: a walnut notary's desk, a bookcase with open shelves, desolately empty, and a round mahogany table. The bed was immense and black, made of wrought iron with brass knobs; opposite stood a tiny marble fireplace, of unidentifiable period, strangely placed between two large windows that looked out over sloping roof-tops towards the mainland. In a sunny moment the previous afternoon he had seen the rosy glimmer of the lagoon reflecting the light and, beyond the lagoon, a long strip that could have been either land or fog. Even the red gleam on the water and the dark strip at the side seemed to him saturated by metaphysical cold.

Later, going into the bathroom, he had seen the old

enamel tub stained with high-water marks of indelible antiquity. How foolish! he had said to himself. To settle into this dreadful house only because she had given him the address. He could have stayed in a good hotel for barely twice what he was paying here.

He looked at the blazing fire to console himself, and it seemed to flare up awkwardly, feebly and even with a shiver. 'But this wood is chestnut!' he exclaimed with irritation.

It was just two o'clock. After spending the entire morning visiting churches, focusing his gaze on immense paintings far away in the darkness, he was tired and had a headache. He would willingly have stretched out on his bed for an hour, but the cold had by now made itself tactile. He rubbed his numb fingers together and decided it would be better to go back to the Piazza and settle in one of the well-heated cafés.

No one goes to Venice in the winter! he continued to repeat to himself in the deserted *calli*, in the course of the twenty minutes it took to get to the Piazza. Wouldn't he at least see her this evening? It was barely half a promise: If I manage to get away from my old friends, she had told him, I'll stop by the café (the last one on the right, facing San Marco ... I can never remember names) at four-fifteen. If you don't see me then, you will have to excuse me. We will see each other another evening. I always go to the café at four-fifteen if I can.

He crossed the Piazza diagonally, almost intent on coming to terms, geometrically, not so much with the Piazza itself as with the external world: the world of objectives, intentions and projects. But what was he talking about? These intentions were mere shapes in the fog, rather than projects: pious intentions – not even so very pious, to tell the truth, to the extent that they concerned a woman. How to behave – this was the problem. He had become confused as soon as he stopped dealing in timber. If only everything could be reduced to the simplicity of a contract, he said to himself, knowing perfectly well that the comparison was lame.

Contract was not the right term to convey the meaning he intended; rather it was simplicity. Let's call it geometrical simplicity, he decided. Or let's say it's easier to make land surveys and appraisals than to have a relationship with a woman.

But what's driving me? he asked himself almost angrily. It seemed unjust to him that external reality should present itself to him in such a disturbing way. 'The world should merely be measured,' he exclaimed, making a sweeping gesture with his arms, 'not scrutinized anxiously, fearfully, even with shame.' He was humiliated at being in Venice, ashamed of pacing back and forth across the Piazza with long steps, like a gallant. At his age it was unthinkable to importune a woman; almost any other silliness would be more dignified. Well now, he thought, trying to calm himself, this Piazza has stayed the same for centuries through the most extraordinary vicissitudes, insisting only on two essential properties: dimension and form. Isn't this just what one should look out for? Why would anything survive except as testimony to the imperturbable sameness of the world? Isn't that why I am in Venice?

31

This surveyor's insight, he recognized, was more mystical-escapist than practical. And yet, in spite of the damp, the cold, the heavy sky and occasional blasts of irritating wind, the Piazza helped him by virtue of its geometry, or in some other way: almost an acre in area, with scattered groups of pigeons and wrapped-up figures moving across it, long unchartable lines, but all enclosed within a rectangular space. Sometimes the clouds above parted, letting narrow segments of sky show through: an unexpected blue, made pale by a windy winter evening, in which everything without exception seemed to be heading towards night and solitude. And then at once the Piazza overcame the least definite of the changes in the sky, bringing him back to the simplest meteorological version which allowed no questions or qualifications. Indeed by its exclusive geometry the rectangle of the Piazza imposed a discipline of not thinking. Except for dogs that piss against trees! he said to himself. No matter how simple it may be, no proposition can achieve the simplicity of a rectangle.

He looked again at the Piazza, almost gratefully, but the scene seemed to change: now the swarming pigeons seemed to be miserable refugees from the Beyond, waiting for municipal hand-outs, precisely in the person of a bespectacled and haughty young man scattering handfuls of bird seed. They too are exiles from the unwelcoming blur of the sky and the dark variables of the clouds, he thought, searching for the mainland, resigned provisionally to accepting the miserable bounty of the Piazza, appearing to want to appease their gullets more than to satisfy their souls. Where else would they have gone? A whole roster of names of cities came to mind, from Aberdeen to Toulon, but in none of them did a winter evening appear to be more agreeable or the place more generously forthcoming than Venice. Yet this flight from uncertainty, from confusion, from complication, like any taking refuge or reducing to the simplest terms, merely meant adapting to the wretched monotony of survival, rather than salvation; one went on from one day to the next merely to prolong one's life. So one could say with almost absolute certainty that the dogs in the world continued day after day to piss on trees. How much longer? he asked himself.

Once in a café in Turin a busy waiter with long legs and arms crossed had stationed himself against a pillar in front of his table. The waiter's face was traversed by inscrutable thoughts, which rendered it darkly tender.

'How much time is lost!' he had said. The waiter had looked at him, affably questioning.

He continued, 'It was once believed that men were created by the seven planets.'

'What do you mean?' the waiter asked. 'Would you like another coffee?'

'Another? Now? What difference would that make?' he replied and stood up, leaving a huge tip in apology, while the baffled waiter watched him. 'I have no time now!' he said as he went away.

Since then, every so often he suspected that the present had only a discontinuous and accidental relation to the past. Sometimes the present appeared to him to be a figure: a position among the planets, nailed so firmly to the celestial vault that after a month or a year he could return there to consult the oracle, receive a sign or some other portent. Even now he thought he could feel the menacing weight of a premonition bear down almost physically on the Piazza.

But where? he asked himself, turning around and tracing the border of the sky with his gaze or, rather, the line of huge cornices, the peaks of the dormer windows, the tops of the chimney-pots. The surroundings seemed immensely oppressive: pigeons too grey, gusts of damp wind, the sound of footsteps, snatches of violin music from the café, every time the doors opened to let someone come in or go out, and suddenly from somewhere, amidst many voices that were misted over or faint, a voice that was clear more out of arrogance than in its timbre: 'Drop dead, imbecile!'

Before he could manage to place it the voice fell silent as abruptly as it had sounded; then out of the unexpected silence other voices slowly began to emerge, more or less indecipherable, more or less distant, in the dimming light of evening.

'You should go to the doctor!' a portly woman said peremptorily to the person with her. She came up to him from the right, shoving her elbow into his stomach and passing him on the left with a baleful look.

For a moment he followed her large legs and black heels marching across the scattered pigeon food.

The instant! he thought, looking at the black heels of the unknown woman. This instant! Now? And then? It's cold now. Where am I going? In the meantime, almost without his being aware of it, as he was turning over thoughts in his mind, it came to him that 'now' was a sort

The Piazzetta, Venice

of interval: neither time nor figure, neither day nor night, neither past nor future, but a bouquet of everything, gathered together to be dedicated with a bow of obeisance, to the creating planets.

At this proposed dedication, the idea of an interval, lazy or idle at first, leaped from the back of his mind towards the proscenium arch. Now the façades on the right towards the campanile seemed to bask in a privileged white light, so that the architectural details shone with unearthly splendour; the glass in the doors, when they occasionally opened, sparkled in the dark of the archways. Every such incident took place in a repeating, non-definitive *mode*: events, instead of replacing one another, seemed to slide one on top of the other, neither opposing or cancelling each other out. With no antecedents and no consequences, everything organized itself cumulatively, according to the precise logic of a deck of cards.

'Shuffling instead of grammar!' he said, satisfied with his invention: it was a minor satisfaction. He was content, certainly, but with a minor contentment. More modestly, he could have said that the hour, the instant, the present, whatever logic it brought, was for him a way of observing things patiently, without anticipation or prejudice, a mode freed from trying to listen, hoping for the best, and without fearing the worst, as one listens to an orchestra while the instruments are being tuned: hearing, pretending not to hear, or at least overlooking any discordant sounds so as to pay attention to the essential.

What essential? he asked himself. No matter how hard he tried, he thought, he always returned to the idea of an

36

interval, a postponement, in an ever more anxious attempt to pass from the anxiety of uncertainty and confusion to a neutrality, probably benevolent, of the same uncertainty. He flung out his arms with a gesture of ironic resignation. 'Virtue lies in the middle way!' he exclaimed. His virtue was not by nature in mediating, but in renouncing: he didn't say 'And this is that!' but rather: 'Neither this nor that.' Only in negation did he feel that the ambiguity of thought, the same ambiguity of expression and also of images and sounds, through which he was always constrained to think, could, if not disappear or vanish, at least provisionally appease itself in equable indifference.

Now darkness was falling quickly; the great church, oppressed by shadows, gathered itself up as if in a hurry to set off into the dark, while the Piazza lamented its departure with futile screeches from violins. And now! The cupolas were already dark and the pigeons lined up in the little light that remained and dedicated themselves to collective defecation with almost Muslim discipline.

'That bodes ill!' he commented, shaking his head.

It was now ten minutes past four. He continued to shake his head as he moved towards the café. With omens like these she certainly won't come! he said to himself, pushing the café door.

But there she was, incredibly enough, present in flesh and blood and verifiable in every possible way, even to her ugly pallor.

'Do you see I have come?' she said with a vague smile, avoiding the two hands he had instinctively extended towards her. 'Who knows what you will think of me!' she added, with an expression of displeasure.

'Why?' he asked.

She bowed her head. 'Well,' she began, suddenly looking up at him, 'who knows what you would have thought if I hadn't come?'

'I don't know,' he admitted.

They moved to an empty table by the window and took off their coats, which an attentive waiter hurried to take from them and then solemnly bore off on his arm to an unknown destination.

'Well!' she said, 'It is real sable. I hope there won't be any mix-up.'

'I'll go and get it,' he said, standing up, but she stopped him, holding on to his sleeve.

'No! They know perfectly well how to handle fur coats.'

At that moment the waiter returned. They ordered tea and cakes, without mentioning the coat.

'You are elegant,' he complimented her after a certain interval of silence. 'Very elegant.'

She smiled. 'That's not true. I am completely unfashionable.' Then, without paying attention to what he was saying to her, she began to explain that in such dreadful weather she had been convinced she would not come to meet him. She had come to the café only to see whether her hypothesis, that he had already left Venice, corresponded with the truth.

'And on the contrary,' he said, 'as you see, I have stayed.'

'I hope that you haven't stayed on my account,' she began, 'that is, to keep our appointment. That would have been truly silly.'

'I don't like leaving,' he declared. 'What's more I don't even like arriving.'

'Oh, really! Then how can you say you like travelling?'

'I am not talking about travel,' he explained, 'or at least not only about travel. I am referring to my general attitude, as far as words, speeches, premisses, conclusions are concerned. . . .'

'Words?' she asked.

'Yes, words,' he confirmed. 'Words, but also every expression, whether it is verbal or not. How can I say it? Even a musical phrase, a figure in a painting has a double meaning: that of departure (that is of understanding each other, from which one begins to think) and that of arrival. Arriving at that, there is nothing more to think about. Exemplary expressions of grammar belong to this last category of arrival, such as: The dog pisses against the tree! Remember?'

She nodded.

'And yet the problem is that these two categories of arrival and departure are never separate and not really distinct,' he continued, 'and in fact even the simplest phrase, just below the declarative threshold, one manifestly requiring no thought, conceals another which appears to be the real station for departure, when one looks closely.'

'An airport, perhaps?'

He smiled: 'An airport certainly!'

She bent over her cup of tea.

'Do you know,' she mused after a few minutes of silence, 'perhaps I am less stupid than I appear to be. I think I partly understand what you are saying, but what I understand makes me uneasy; I should even say it disturbs me.'

Silence returned, this time almost a physical obstruction. Through the window – there where, moving his head slightly, the shadow he cast blocked the reflection of the light from within – only a small part of the Piazza could be seen, full of a darkness and a silence as inhospitable as a desert, no matter how many people were passing by. The silence between them appeared to have raised the curtain on the silence in the Piazza beyond the window, with an almost precipitate decision that now seemed to him irrevocable.

And yet she slowly began to speak again: 'That way of saying things, mine, I mean – I am speaking of my way, which above all falsifies what I am thinking and ruins everything.'

'No,' he intervened. 'You are actually right.'

'Right?' she asked, almost with hostility. 'Of course I am right! However, I should have made it clear that it is not you that makes me uneasy, but the fact that the part I understand of what you are saying, I understand because I already knew it. As far as I can tell, you are discovering the umbrella, in a certain sense. It is also true, however, that before you discovered it, that umbrella was invisible to me; in other words I lacked the experience of what I knew. See how many beautiful speeches without conclusions I too can make?'

'And yet I have never heard a more well-constructed speech,' he said, laughing and clapping his hands.

The waiter approached their table. 'Very well, bring me a cognac,' he said, not knowing what to say.

The bridge

As soon as the waiter had gone, he commented, 'How silly! Why would I ever order a cognac?'

She looked dubious at first and then burst into unexpected and strangely resonant laughter; actually into a laugh so loud that everyone in the room turned round, except for the waiters.

'I would be happy if you would have dinner with me this evening,' he said.

'And I am happy to accept,' she said.

From then on they had dinner together every evening except for one time when she met him at the café to tell him that that evening she couldn't be with him: her friends were ill and she hadn't the heart to leave them. Then he went with her to the chemists.

'You know, every time she is ill he runs a temperature,' she told him. 'I suspect he plays games with the thermometer.' She went on, telling him about these two old people: he, at eighty, as solid and gloomy as a tower, had been a famous musician. Twenty years before he had left his society wife, who was sophisticated and rich, to live with a forty-year-old piano teacher who was poor, retiring and ailing; she, the piano teacher, as time passed, had become ever more ailing, more delicate and retiring, but in her way also more beautiful. 'Do you know the strangest thing? His wife has always provided for them. When she died five years ago, she left to them both the house in which they live and a generous income for life, even naming the woman explicitly.'

'What a fine person!' he commented.

Later, near the door of her friends' house, he asked:

'Can I see you tomorrow?' She replied that it would be impossible. But the next evening she joined him at the restaurant, when he had almost begun to eat, excusing herself for being late as if she had forgotten saying she couldn't join him. The triumph of habit which this forget-fulness implied made him happy: he had never before felt himself so naturally taken for granted, and every so often, without saying a word, he raised his eyes to look at her, content in the certainty of finding her near him.

Unexpectedly he felt great curiosity about the friends with whom she was staying.

'They have often urged me to invite you!' she said.

'Why have you never done so?'

She shook her head. 'They are a bit gossipy and espe-cially jealous of anyone I am with.' Then she tried to crack a walnut. Holding the nutcracker with both hands, she pressed her elbows against the table and suddenly the nut exploded, and a big piece flew into her glass, splashing the wine.

'Well done!' he cried. They looked at each other a moment and both suddenly burst out laughing.

She started over. 'The trouble is that I love them dearly and yet I can't endure them: they remind me of my child-hood, my mother, whom I loved unreservedly, and other things I don't wish to remember. Things I would prefer never to have happened. Do you understand? No, that doesn't make sense. I mean, the thing I really don't want is to feel that my life is only "afterwards", that is, after the death of my father or after that of my mother, or rather even more precisely after the death of my aunt. May I tell you?' she continued after an instant of silence. 'Every time I arrive all three of them surround me as if they had been doing nothing for months but wait for me.'

'All three who?' he asked.

'Including the dog!' she said, laughing. 'Don't you remember the dog I told you about? My dog? He's the one. This is the scene: the maid ushers me into the drawing-room, a finger at her lips to signal me to keep silent; and when I arrive in the centre by the round table, with all my luggage, she begins to shout, "Guess who's here! See who's here!" Then the two old people appear at the same moment, each from his or her own room, and the dog arrives skating along the hall from the kitchen, where he stays.'

'Magnificent!' he said. 'So the old man and the old woman and the dog each spend their time in their own way and come together on the occasion of your arrival?'

'That's true. That is the impression they give,' she exclaimed.

They drank their coffee silently. 'They have no right,' he said. 'You could of course sell the dog. Why did you tell them about me?'

She didn't reply.

'I was only joking,' he said again, after a while. 'But I understand your situation: it is not very amusing!'

She shrugged. 'It is certainly not amusing,' she admitted, 'but what in the world is ever amusing, except for certain funerals, and of course you?'

'Am I amusing?' He was stupefied.

She scrutinized him in deliberate detail. 'Perhaps it's

your eyebrows,' she said. 'Or, let's say that you entertain me. Tell me something about yourself.' She paused. 'Your family, for instance . . .'

'Timber – they were concerned with timber. Not very entertaining.'

'Were they in the timber business?'

He shrugged. 'My father started it, after various attempts in other directions. Even with wood,' he continued after a moment of silence, 'he was not a great success. He would buy wood at ten and, after various efforts, procrastination and meditation, sell it again at eight. He thought he was the most astute of business men; in fact, he once succeeded in buying a load of timber from a carpenter's shop at two and selling it again at twelve. Well, they hauled him into court and made him pay fines, damages and almost sent him to jail: the wood was rotten, but he hadn't realized it. In other words, I knew more about wood when I was twelve than he did. He often took me with him to warehouses and into the forest, without ever paying attention to what I said: Don't act smart! was the most he would say.'

'Did you like the forest?' she asked, after a few minutes of silence.

He shrugged. 'There is forest and forest,' he said. 'I remember some very beautiful ones. Pine forests! you may say. But you see, there are pine trees and pine trees. The ones I mean are slender, tall and flexible: they look like a giant's ladder that needs only a few branches to reach the clouds, wind, and sky, not a dense tangle of growth that limits its height. And what wood! Few branches means

The Riva

few knots.'

'In other words you don't lose sight of the wood,' she said.

'Certainly,' he admitted, 'wood is only wood, but one must know something before getting into it. Few things, very few, but they make all the difference in the value.'

They were silent for a while.

'And your mother?' she asked. 'Was she beautiful?'

He opened his arms. 'I wished,' he said, 'if you only knew how I wished she were beautiful and also intelligent. Sometimes I thought: If instead of saying what she said the way she said it, she had said it in this other way, it would have been much better: in other words I tried to improve, not so much the thought as the literary presentation of the thought, but it was a wasted effort; she persevered in her stupidity. . . . She merely repeated everything my father said, using exactly the same haphazard grammar. What was special to her was a doleful look, which I thought made her eyes, those large black eyes that drooped naturally, droop even more to the side. Because her eyes were slanted sideways, her lamentations appeared to make private things public, a sort of official declaration of disaster. What's more, I believe that, apart from sadness, even beauty, ugliness, stupidity and intelligence are public attitudes. My father seemed to have understood that when he told me not to act smart. He said it with a wink and she repeated it with a sob. Poor creature! I loved her deeply. My great love for her was never returned.'

'How do you know?' she interrupted him. 'Your mother may have loved you greatly but she may have been too

48

reserved, too shy to let you know.'

'No,' he replied, 'I know. My mother loved only my father. When he died sitting at a table in the café where he had gone to discuss who-knows-what business deal, she absented herself; she was no longer either stupid, intelligent, beautiful, ugly, or doleful, but a sort of walking vacancy, as vast as the universe.'

They were silent. He swished the cognac in his glass, she poked at crumbs on the tablecloth.

He continued. 'Then I understood what that emptiness was: a question, nothing but a question.'

'Yes?'

'You see,' he explained, 'after my father's death I worked very hard to get the wreck back into working order. I managed to pay off the debts and even to collect some of the money owed. It took me a year and a half to do that, and, I should add, much skill, many compromises and manoeuvres. When I thought I could say, Very well! We have brought the ship into harbour, she died as he had done – suddenly, seated at a table, but in the kitchen, not in a bar. And here is the emptiness. Here is the question: What shall I do about it? What good does it do? Not so much concrete things . . . not the business, the house, as far as I know. Nothing of all this, but my love for her. The love that I had felt for her as long as I can remember no longer served. Very well! So then I too went away. I have never returned. I am a practical man. What good would it do to return?'

'Yes!' she said, nodding her head in approval.

'A little cognac would be good for you. . . .' he proposed. 'It would give you rosy cheeks.'

'If it is only for that,' she protested, 'I could always resort to paint. Do you know the fiery red cheeks of those Russian dolls? Is that what you want?'

He laughed. 'How could I dare to want something?'

She stood up. 'Have you finished your cognac?' she asked peremptorily.

He apologized, and then also stood up.

'Don't keep on apologizing,' she said as they were leaving. 'Are you my friend? A friend has the right to want what he likes and not to want what he doesn't like.'

'That,' he said, bowing, 'is the Magna Carta of friendship.'

3

They began to touch, or rather he impulsively took her
hand, at first without thinking about it. She was laughing,
and without even drawing back continued to laugh, but
the laugh had a different sound. The insignificance of the
spontaneous gesture was thus replaced by an undefined
intention, a vague feeling began to take shape between
them as a shared understanding. He released her hand
slowly, looking out of the window towards the Piazza.

People wearing heavy coats were still crossing in all
directions; there was a sense of leave-taking, soft and
heavy.

'Winter is about to end,' he said.

'Yes. It is still cold, but one can feel it in the air. . . .
My dog wants to go to the country,' she said.

He made a gesture of impatience: 'One mustn't pay too
much attention to animals. They never know what they
want.'

'Do you know?' she asked.

That evening she said she couldn't have dinner with him,
and they parted glumly.

He stayed on in the café, at the same table, seated in the same chair, looking out of the same window past the portico. 'Before and after,' he repeated, trying to grasp the sense of the phrase, the difference between 'before' and 'after', and the desolation that this difference implied.

'Before and after' was actually in some ways the desolation of the difference, which he now felt in the movement, the whole surface of his life: sometimes imperceptible, sometimes deep as a crevasse. That difference was not only what it now appeared to be, but invoked the whole past.

'To hell with it!' he said, banging his fist on the marble. 'After all, she didn't have to leave her pretty little fingers in mine.'

Suddenly appeased, he smiled at the idea of the diminutive 'pretty little fingers' and thought that her hands were on the large side rather than small, perhaps even too bony and too long in relation to her body. Or perhaps not? Her legs, for example, for all he could see of them, would be considered long; in fact, although she was at least a hand's breadth shorter than he, at the level of the pelvis, the difference seemed less to him; moreover, measurements apart, her legs bent, crossed and moved like long legs. All right, he concluded. Long legs. And yet, he thought uncertainly, that did not imply that the rest of her body was compressed or foreshortened. He thought its proportions were elegant, even if somehow illogical. Her body was not small, but rather bony and long, with a certain solidity – especially long. Each part of it looked long, that is, but altogether it looked short, or if not actually short, certainly shorter than

Quiet canal

his body, which could not be called very long. And logic? he asked himself. Where was logic?

How foolish! he thought, striking his forehead with his hand. It was certainly not a question of plane geometry. The width of a woman's body was seen at various levels; so a detail, which could seem delicate, nevertheless gave an impression of being solid because of its concealed width. That is why there are so-called falsely thin people.

It was not very convincing, but he felt this phrase 'falsely thin people' offered him a tool for investigation. He began turning her body around in his mind, trying to make it correspond to his notion of false-thinness, making one part fuller and another more slender until, whichever way he looked at it, amidst the conjurings of his imagination, *proditum visit sine nube corpus.*

'Oh, look here!' he said to himself, astonished. He looked about for distraction and noticed that with the advance of winter, the café had lost its elegant air; now there was music only on Sundays; the long winter afternoons were now swathed in silence, the lights were low and the waiters' activity less formal – or flamboyantly noisy. He liked this. The two of them could talk or not with confident naturalness; the nonchalant silence of the café chimed with their own dark or ambiguous corners of silence. But now, alone, looking at the intimacy of the frivolous, semi-dark setting, he thought he perceived an implicitly permissive atmosphere, a note of discreet compliance. After all, he thought, how many provincial hotels exhibit the same dated luxury, the same worn carpets, the ornate silverware, threadbare upholstery and faded colours in the same conventional mode, emblems with a prescribed iconography of a grand brothel? But look here! he repeated with a mixture of discomfort and rage. The weight of knowledge of the little world or, rather, *demi-monde* of semi-luxurious prostitutes oppressed him. Certainly that world wasn't his and she was not a prostitute, but innocently, out of stupidity and without realizing it, they had ended up in a blind alley, in the suffocating confines of a relationship that could be called ambiguous if not explicitly vulgar, in disarming old Venice. But look here! he said to himself again, banging his fist on the marble. And who was she? She was certainly not a young girl or a fragile woman who could be considered in thrall to abstract yearnings, bending over the pages of Baudelaire in the pale light of a night lamp. She was too sure of herself – sometimes even arrogant, it might be said. She allowed herself to have fun with him and at his expense, to assume a note of superiority or to seem to give way with tolerant detachment, when she wasn't viewing him in a protective way. Thinking now about her, everything about her seemed offensive, if not deliberately irritating. She is hateful, he decided; she lacks sensibility, intuition, perhaps she isn't even intelligent. And then – he added spitefully – even physically she's not much. Aside from her pallor, or perhaps that made it more evident, there were subtle traces of weariness around her eyes, hinting that the shadows out of which her glance had emerged would soon prevail. The evening before, while she was laughing, her mouth had seemed to yield to some unlooked-for abandon; her hands, which she kept in view on the white tablecloth, suddenly became opaque; or at least the pallor of her skin against the white linen revealed its ephemeral quality; one could perceive that an inexorable process had already set in, that her skin would become thinner, her knuckles more prominent, and eventually her veins more exposed.

He bowed his head, seized by unexpected discomfort. He would have consoled her if he had been able to. They would have travelled together to see unfamiliar cities: Prague, for example. Or to distract her he would have returned, with her, to find the sheep of Skipton again. If he could, he would have embraced her, or at least put his jacket over her shoulders, if one summer evening she had gone out too lightly dressed and become chilled.

But what am I saying? What am I doing? he suddenly asked himself. He put his elbows on the table, pressed his hands against his temples and closed his eyes. What am I doing? he repeated. What am I in the process of doing? He remained silent with his eyes closed until he felt a touch on his shoulder. He thought it was the waiter; he turned irritably, ready to argue.

It was she. 'Excuse me,' she said. 'I've returned. I didn't want to leave you so brusquely.'

Without saying anything, without even standing, he smiled at her. 'Have you ever been to Prague?' he asked.

'Prague?' she said, sitting as she usually did, facing him across the table. 'Not to Prague. Why do you ask?'

'They say it is a marvellous city,' he said. 'I've never seen it, but in a certain sense it is familiar to me. When I am in a crisis, I think of going to Prague, and for days I go about the streets and squares of that unknown city. Of course I'm day-dreaming. Now, crisis after crisis, I find myself at the street corner where I was last time I left to return to my senses.'

'Why are you in crisis now?' she asked.

He shrugged. 'I don't know. Perhaps a bit because of you. Can I risk saying so?'

She nodded. After a pause she said, 'You know, I am glad I have found you still here. Otherwise I wouldn't have known where to look for you. Who knows where you go when you aren't with me?'

'Secrets to keep from ladies!' He laughed. But suddenly he stopped laughing, and said, 'How absurd! Where could I go? Venice is a prison.'

She looked at him thoughtfully. 'At certain moments every place seems to be a prison,' she said. 'If I think back on it, my life has often been a prison too: my childhood, for example. Yet the prison walls protect and I already knew that then; if I spoke quietly, if I walked on tiptoe, if I lurked in corners it was because I was afraid of being discovered and flung outside the prison, into the open world.'

'What sort of child were you?' he asked, taking one of her hands again. He regretted the gesture immediately and started to withdraw his own hand, but this time she held on to it.

'Do you want my hand or don't you?' she asked.

They both burst out laughing.

She continued, 'I often tell myself the story of my life

or at least of my childhood. When I am in crisis, instead of going to Prague as you do, I get drunk and begin *ab ovo*, that is, from the beginning, just like any respectable biography.'

'Does this console you?' he asked.

'Does Prague console you?' she rejoined. 'Only I am seeking not consolation, but a comparison; I believe my life doesn't exist in this or any other isolated moment, but by comparison with itself. It is in fact not even the past that counts, but, so to speak, the sameness of the comparison. . . . The comparison I am talking about tells me that after all, today as well as yesterday is part of the same life and therefore there is no reason for me to be surprised or to complain. You see,' she added after a moment, 'the other time, when you spoke of your mother, I wasn't thinking only about your childhood, of distant events, another past, but of you, the man you are today. What you told me, in other words, was not a variation on yourself but, quite the contrary, a confirmation that you are the same person today.'

He shook his head. 'No. I don't believe in the continuity of individuals; anyway, apart from, or contrary to every theoretical reason, I must admit that my curiosity about your past is limitless.'

'Well, it is certainly possible that you are pretending to be curious only out of politeness,' she said. 'And then, apart from that, I should at least be drunk.' She shook her head. 'Or,' she hesitated, 'I could pretend to be drunk. We could drink champagne and, if you don't interrupt me with one of your too refined kindnesses, I could try to speak to

Ponte del Piovan

you as solemnly as I speak to myself.'

'Oh! Do you speak solemnly to yourself?' he said.

'Certainly! Just like your sheep!' she replied. 'Doesn't talking to oneself imply an intention to be truthful? And isn't truth a solemn concept? How else could it be defined, unless one assumes solemnity?'

'I agree,' he conceded. 'But perhaps it's better to speak solemn truths than the silly things I usually say about truth and language. But, to be practical, in the case of solemn wines, do you prefer sweet or dry?'

They called a waiter and after some hesitation permitted themselves to order champagne, of a good year, if not excessively expensive. Both found it excellent to begin with and very bad by the end of the bottle.

In any case, after the first glass, she turned with a deliberately theatrical gesture towards the end of the room, and fixed her eyes on the great blackened mirror. Without deigning to look at him again, she began to speak and he listened in ceremonious and even reverent silence.

'I was born on April the twelfth. My mother sometimes told me the day I was born was rainy and unseasonably cold; at other times she said it was a sunny day and the peach trees along the road were in blossom: white flowers, that gave the effect of a snowfall, she said. I suppose that these contradictory details had also been told to her; or it is possible that both descriptions were partially true, in other words that it was raining but because of all the white blossoms on the trees, the rain gave the effect of an unseasonal snowfall.

'In any case, this dual scenario of my birth, artificial as

it may be, became as time passed one of my most secure memories. Another secure memory, but more spontaneous, is of my father, a person I must have seen very infrequently because, my mother said, he was a sea captain who lived at the port of origin of his ship, that is, Venice; or as my aunt later told me, he was a famous lawyer whose chambers were in Venice, but who owned a great deal of land where we lived: a big farm and the house we lived in. In any case he was rich, and we lacked for nothing. Before his death I remember our house in the country had a beautiful orchard that bore lots of apples; the rooms were filled with fine furniture, some of which was later sold, and we had much silver, which I subsequently sold.

'But what I remember most precisely is the floor of one of the rooms of our apartment in town: a parquet with great squares of dark wood, framed with strips of paler wood and on this a pair of black shoes: the shoes of my father, and consequently also the person of my father, whose feet were obviously inside the shoes. Light came in from the balcony, almost white because of the pale transparent curtains that moved in the morning breeze. There were few people on the street, and of those few, some had stopped to talk on the pavement just in front of the house, by the window of the shop where my aunt sold sheets, tablecloths and other household linen.

'In another memory, more confused – perhaps it wasn't morning, but evening – light came not from the balcony but from a lamp of white glass, and it wasn't parquet I saw but a carpet, under the table where I was on my hands and knees. In any case I still remember my father or at least his black shoes and his way of speaking, which was clear and to the point, while my mother sometimes wept quietly with her hands over her eyes, seated or perhaps lying on a sofa in a corner; at other times she complained in a loud voice, walking back and forth in the room.

'I also remember the silence surrounding these voices: the pauses in which one heard the squeaking of a distant door or a few words spoken in another room.

'Because the door on to the stairs was often open on these occasions, I would go down into the courtyard, which was small and quite dark, and hide there for some time behind a big chest full of coal, with a cane in my hand or a stick to poke at the boy who tended the furnace, every time he came into the courtyard to get coal or something else. In response the boy would seize me and lift me up above his head, growling menacingly. There was also a cat with red stripes which came holding its tail up straight while the boy turned around holding me high above his head with his arms straight, and I could see the roof-tops of the houses whirling against the sky, almost borne away by the wind. These images of the strange cat, of being borne up in the arms of the furnace boy, of my father's black shoes, all mixed and blended into a unity, which to be precise could be filed under each of these headings – but I call it "memory of my father" because I have no other memory of him.

'The images connected with the word "patience" are a different sort: yellow trees, for example, or a huge terra-cotta jar with a cover made of wood, that was supposed to have come from the South. Kitchen things above all:

the kitchen, the one in the house in town, was long and rather narrow. It was there, especially when it was raining, that we talked about patience, that universal remedy for incurable ills. Even now rain and patience are often linked together in my imagination, especially long and slow autumn rain.

'When I was grown, the house in town and my aunt's shop vanished, and we went to live in the country with another aunt, old and hairy, who reeked of sardines; she was a cousin on my father's side of the family. The first aunt had taken an apartment and a smaller shop, but she no longer came to see us. My mother sometimes went to visit her in the afternoon, secretly, each time making signs, her finger to her lips, for me to keep silent about it. What is important, she told me on these occasions, is freedom from need; all the rest is secondary.

'There was always an air of morality about my mother. She would deliver long lectures on poverty and religion: Lord! she often recited, repeating the prayer of Hagar, Condemn me not to poverty lest I steal, and also gave long commentaries on this prayer. Her principal argument in this equation of poverty with stealing was that the stealing was never as easy as poverty, because the last was a judgement of fate, while stealing involved personal initiative: in other words, it was a virtue, and to practise it required a number of intellectual and moral qualities, from cleverness to courage to firm deliberation.

'While my father was alive we lacked for nothing. My father had sold the house, orchard and some shops in town to my mother, but after my father's death the income from the property was assigned to this maternal aunt who, among other things, soon began to drool, and later became incontinent and pissed everywhere.

'But it happened, somewhat later, that some other relatives who were our enemies claimed responsibility for this aunt and wanted her to live near them; and after many quarrels and prolonged negotiation, they obtained a court order in their favour. I don't remember the details. I do remember my mother explaining, often at great length, that if the old woman were moved it would mean the loss of our income and perhaps also our eviction: in a word, our ruin. I remember this word "ruin" having a sound of great solemnity.

'The sun rose and set, summer passed: the word "ruin" persisted almost as if it were the ultimate reality of heaven and earth. Wherever one looked one thought: Here is ruin! It cast a sort of shadow that drained colours of their brightness and insinuated itself into any conversation we were having, so that, to adapt to the severity of this ever-threatening ruin, we felt constrained to speak in whispers and almost to hide ourselves, every time anything even remotely agreeable happened.

'One day, while we were sitting in the garden, all but bent double under the weight of this impending ruin, my mother suddenly sat up straight. My dear, she said, in a voice she seemed to have retrieved from years before, as though borrowing it from the past for a special occasion, Your aunt is not well! She needs a doctor.

'I was eleven then, and although I had had my first academic success, I had worked long and hard at my

S. Biagio

studies, and certainly couldn't be called highly intelligent. My mother even claimed that I understood nothing at all. But her special voice that day ushered me into a new world, strewn with fears and uncertainties, but a world of courage and firm determination, in which for the first time things seemed clear, so that I felt I too had the intelligence to grasp them. What bothered me about this relationship between subjective intelligence and objective clarity was the tranquil indifference along with the excessive simplicity of the things around me: I saw things, that is, with a quiet concern, with a kind of lucid anxiety that afterwards, in different degrees depending on the circumstances, never left me. But let's forget about afterwards. At the time this volte-face of the world seemed to me magical: it was the force of destiny, fate made flesh, that took the stage in place of talk – or luck.

'To be brief, I will say only that my mother, without explaining the details of her decision, instructed me to wait until the doctor had examined my aunt and was talking to my mother on the ground floor, then to accompany my aunt to the top of the stairs and leave her there on her own. Now this aunt was very docile, although she pissed and shat everywhere like an animal; the touch of a fingertip was all that was needed, she would follow with great joy, grinning so happily that her dentures often fell from her mouth, together with a stream of drool.

'I remember every detail of her dentures vividly, because of the difficulties, different each time, of adjusting them in her mouth: her thick tongue lolled sideways in always unpredictable ways. This time you won't have to put in her teeth, my mother said.

'But even that time her teeth fell out in the course of the short walk from the edge of her bed to the top of the stairs. I paid no attention, however, leaving her toothless, with her tongue hanging out and one foot half-way off the top step. She wobbled, swaying forward and backward, and more often forward than back, until, almost by degrees, she decided to proceed, and raising her foot over the void, almost to the height of her other knee, she got it tangled in her clothes and fell head first down the stairs with a grunt of joy.

'I was near her and watched over her preparatory moves. I saw her take off, so to speak, with that expansive joy in her eyes and her lolling tongue and cascade of drool. Instead of returning to my room as my mother had instructed, I hurled myself in front of her. In fact she fell on top of me, and instead of my stopping her, after first bouncing on her head she tumbled down over the banister on to the ground floor. So I broke my leg and spent a month or more in hospital.

'I remember little about that time except that, despite the nuisance of my leg, I immediately felt great serenity, or rather, instead of serenity (which might be misunderstood) the stillness of astonishment at that change in the world of which I have spoken. But perhaps one ought to say that there is always a point at which the most overwhelming passion becomes mere anxious indifference, tedious pain, serene as the famous force of destiny. Perhaps that is typical of convalescence: in hospital, every afternoon, I saw my mother smiling at me on one side of the bed, and turning the other way I saw other beds, other patients and nurses carrying out their usual activities, smiling and giving medicine, or walking about severely and sadly with bedpans and clysters. Between these activities, in spite of their variety and my mother's smile, there was a bond, a relationship; or rather they had the same foundation. And finally the solidity of this foundation yielded boredom, a sense of the emptiness and transparency of space, of light, of movement, but also a simple tranquillity and a great desire for sleep, abandon, I daresay even for death.

'That's the trouble with all hospitals! you may say. It's true. But even when we went home, my mother and I (she had stayed in a hotel nearby while I was in hospital), this foundation of quiet remained intact. As I was saying, it is a solid foundation, which can accommodate contrast – the noise and conversation in the hospital, but also the silence at home, the solemnity of the unspoken, as well as my present autobiographical tale; it has essentially the same peaceful structure now as it had then.

'What's more, this mania of mine for telling stories in silence does not necessarily amount to autobiography. In a certain atmosphere habitual or even highly predictable things happen day after day, this almost invariable sequence seems to obey the logic of story-telling, although no one speaks. Let's say certain afternoons, even now, present themselves as a story without an author. Even then I felt that certain sounds, certain events were not merely taking place physically, but alluded to other events; and although the allusion was completely unknown to me, the mere fact that everything that happened, however minute or irrelevant, positioned itself on a plane of allusion with every other detail, gave it the rhythm of a story.

'Of course we were never completely silent; my mother actually spoke frequently. But I had the impression that whatever was said, instead of stating the meaning it clearly had, was waiting for another meaning to surface. For example, she said, when she was mending a carpet: Well, it is hard to find wool like this today. And so wool, the word, or perhaps the image, found itself immediately in a storage place for rare narrative objects which were as difficult to find as the wool my mother had been speaking about. And so it happened with the most distracting sounds, the creak of a door or certain musical notes I tried on the piano, and for things even without sound, like the soft tread of the cat. How to tell a story openly about these things in fact? And yet, keeping silent about them, everything carefully repositioned itself in the thesaurus of the novel in progress, with the novelist missing.

'What is important, I told myself, reasonably content, is not to stop, and things in fact follow suit: my mother talked about the border, mending the tablecloth; I touched the keyboard; the cat awoke and, stretching, came towards one of us; the door creaked and opened of itself because of the wood's naturally elastic properties. I thought, She is the one who moves on, leaving us in her wake! And although I knew she was dead, in this silence and stillness the actuality of the out-of-date seemed entirely plausible to me.

'Is it raining? I asked. But there was no answer: in the

first place because the dead don't answer, and in the second place because it wasn't raining at all, but clear, with that wide, almost enamelled sky of early winter. Basically it wasn't important whether it was raining or windy because death would have been able to tell the story of things in its own way; everything, I mean, is available to a voice that's not there. Certainly no one, either living or dead, was speaking then; above all no one was telling a story, but for me at least what I would call a story was in the air, inescapable; it was in fact air, light, sound. Everyone lives within this container: my mother, me, the cat, death, because all that is between us makes a link or a thread or a plot that can be recounted: wind, the rustle of leaves, the low light of winter afternoons, or rain.'

She stopped speaking and they both remained silent for some minutes.

Then she turned to look at him, almost to scrutinize him: 'And everything . . .' she said, 'everything continues to make a plot, my dear friend: Venice, my dog, even you.'

4

Patience! he said to himself, sitting down on the edge of the bed. She will come! Something would come: dawn, sleep, or even she herself would return from her walks in the country with her dog. The weeks passed and now, waking in the silent dark of Venice (or rather, in the special silence that he imagined was common to nights in the Veneto, from Treviso to Padua), he left open all the hypothetical possibilities for coming. Perhaps only the rain would come, the first spring rain, slow but steady, able in a few hours to cleanse the air of the remains of winter fog.

Then it would be full spring – April, perhaps still damp, but already luminous – when she would return at last. Alternatively, he thought, stretching out his legs again under the blankets, she would be able to send him an invitation. If the invitation were the least bit courteous, he would willingly accept it; actually, he admitted, he would accept it with joy.

He closed his eyes. The expression 'joy', to the extent that it occurred accidentally, always produced a set of images which displaced words. He would have said they were images of her, though they were not so much a portrait as a resemblance of a single detail, a gesture and, above all, of her voice, whatever that voice might have been saying: 'Patience!' for example, or 'rain and patience' or another of her favourite expressions – all equally mysterious, equally ambiguous behind their seeming vacuousness.

She is setting these traps to hold on to me, he said suddenly in a rage. But, he asked himself almost in the same breath, what if she doesn't intend to keep me, but rather to let me go? Suddenly words that she had let fall almost absently in conversation, he felt were poles of fundamental opposites in his life: black/white, joy/grief, dog/cat, and so on, in an interminable labyrinth in which he felt lost forever.

He sat up on the edge of the bed again. Ambiguity, he said to himself, nothing but ambiguity. Slowly, imperceptibly, he stopped thinking of how lost he was, to go on framing a vision of her return, describing to himself in ever greater detail how she would appear at the train station in the midst of the crowd. And her dog? Would she have her dog with her? He could already see the huge creature thrusting forward; bracing its back legs, almost strangled by its lead, managing none the less to leap forward panting, and expel its reeking breath right in his face, before he and she managed to shake hands.

For his birthday, she had told him, I promised to take him to the country.

Promised? he had asked.

Well, I let him know we were going; now he is counting on it, she explained. Do you know, on March 25th he will

The balcony

be six years old; he's no longer a puppy.

Yes. But why don't you leave the wretched creature with the old people for good, to keep them company? he replied with irritation.

Wretched creature? How can you call him that if you don't know him, if you haven't ever even seen him? she retorted.

He excused himself crossly. Then they had walked the length of the street in silence.

Listen, why don't you come too? she suddenly proposed, almost at the door of the house. My country place is large: there is space enough for you to do as you please. You can even ignore me, if you feel like it. Or we could have dinner together, as we have done here every evening and this time I will provide it; after all we should take turns, don't you agree?

You are very kind, he replied, hesitating. How long do you plan to stay there?

I don't know, she said, two or three weeks . . . in any case, I must bring the dog back to the old people; they say they can't get along without him, even though they don't pay much attention to him. Yes, do come too!

He had laughed. I'm afraid I can't, he said. No matter how large the house is, I would certainly be a nuisance to the dog.

She let her arm drop. When I said 'you too' I meant the two of us, not you and the dog, she explained.

He shrugged without replying.

You want to make me ashamed of what I've said, she continued, and you are succeeding. But why do you want

74

that? That is my question.

She had turned and without saying goodbye, without even looking at him, vanished into the dark of the entrance.

Ambiguity! he said now to himself, pulling his legs back under the blankets.

It was cold, and daybreak was very far off; there were hours of darkness yet, black as a mirror.

The dog pisses on the mat, he began to recite to himself. Oh, no, he corrected himself. How absurd! It is the cat that pisses on a mat. But this old liking of his for phrases with a meaning that was simple and autonomous no longer even amused him. And anyway, was there really any action, any moment of existence, of dog, cat or of man that could stand alone, definitively enclosed by words? He no longer even trusted in names: for example, 'shoe' certainly referred to footwear; but when, to use the first example that came into his head, he said: She treats me like an old shoe, and 'shoe' became the truest image of his discomfort, did he not also refer to the black mirror of this interminable night? But then did she really treat him like an old shoe? The figure was perhaps exaggerated, he admitted. And anyhow, what could he possibly do about it now?

'Patience,' he said, turning out the light. 'I should try to get some sleep, even if I don't succeed. At least the rain will come!' And he promptly began to imagine, almost drop by drop, the steadiest, heaviest spring downpour possible. What drops! even in the dark, in uncertain light, smooth and translucent as glass, rebounding off every roof and bench and even on the water.

Instead, the shadowy silence of the Veneto persisted without interruption: If the rain should really begin now, he thought, it would have had to start travelling the day before, from the Dolomites, from Treviso, perhaps from the lakes, and still, farther away, from Piemonte. Perhaps at dawn, on the far borders of the Veneto, whole forests of poplars still grey from the winter would be bending with a courteous rustling sound, and villages and towns would be bleached in a silver light. And finally, perhaps at noon, there would be rain in Venice.

What a deluge! he said to himself, thinking he should be able to watch the downpour off the eaves tumble from one storey of the house to another. Even as a child, when the seasonal rains began, he would spend hours at the window, marvelling with his mouth open. Look at him! his mother would say. Here is the boy who sees visions in the grotto! God's innocent. The simpleton from the woods. And to avoid hearing her insults, he would flee towards another, quieter window.

That was quite a different sort of rain. Afterwards, the sky above his native city was not heavy with damp, like the sky over the Veneto, but swept by winds that were transparent and light. How clear everything was then! Perhaps his mind had been as confused then, but clarity had seemed to predominate: his thinking may have been dark and gloomy, but his outlook was crystal-clear; clarity and obscurity, light and dark were not intermingled as they were now, in an ambiguous twilight zone, but each kept to its place. The house was the place of uncertainty and shadows, but outside it, whether morning or evening, the city seemed to speak to him in clear terms. Even at night the sheer legibility of every wall, every tree, shrub and window, the sharpness of the doorways, the projection of the balconies filled him with gratitude and astonishment. The moon permitting, he wandered, content with his astonishment, without desiring or expecting anything other than clarity: a clarity which, without ever deluding him, was apparent everywhere he looked. The moon, in spite of the huge confiding face it showed above the small gardens on the outskirts of town, surveyed the sea on the horizon and the scudding of small distant clouds with metallic severity, while all around was silence and sleeping trees.

On the hill road he would occasionally meet a person who had fled as he had from the window at home. 'I have two cats in my bag,' one of these people once told him, delicately resting the bag on the ground. Nothing happened, so he kicked the bag, which suddenly began to jump, writhe and turn over and over, letting off screeches and howls, until it came to a halt, pulsating, in the shadows of a wall.

Usually he was accompanied by more peaceable creatures: a medium-sized dog which followed him for a long time, sometimes racing ahead of him, and leaping up in front of him suddenly to jab its forepaws confidingly into his stomach. These games and night-time pastimes, which he and the dog silently mocked, ended when the moon set. They always watched this together, seated on the same wall. The moon was caught for an instant in the refracted rays of its own splendour, and then sank below the dazzling silver outline of the hill on their right, and the surrounding shadows and silence immediately revealed their coldness. But in front of them, on the horizon over the sea, the light coming from beyond the hill still shone from innumerable atoms, so that the dominions of light and shade were distinct in the neutral void of the night.

You see? he would say, making as if to survey the difference, looking almost instinctively from one zone to the other: The Lord God has made this! At the time it seemed possible to state the differences. And since the dog appeared to be asking for further elucidation, putting its paws to his face or nipping his fingers, he compared works of mankind (walls, houses, and even, in part, the orchard below) to the works of the Lord (night, clouds, the tranquil starry sky). 'Eius opus sufficiens, meum opus deficiens!' he said, striking himself on the chest. 'Eius opus mirabile, meum opus mutabile,' and so on, comforted by the assent and admiration the dog showed for such Latin clarity of thought.

Finally autumn passed and winter came: the long winter rains. So he and his canine friend had to give up their night-time excursions, and even, when they met, as they did several times a day, they pretended not to know each other. But the wintry rain in the South he felt was more like the rain in the Veneto, not suffused with light as in spring or summer, but relentless and gloomy. Desolate souls, or those who were merely resigned, waited patiently inside their houses, leaving the streets empty. The infrequent passers-by paid no attention to one another, so they often collided. He would prudently turn the corners

Upright Venice

widely, taking care to be able to see as far as the horizon or as the limits of visibility: a curve or the end of a street, often marked by a dingy white patch of fog instead of sky. One inhaled rain, and the sun wasn't even imaginable; the very notion of sun and of time seemed lost, because one no longer knew if the darkness was owing to the rain or the approach of evening. The hours certainly passed, the hands of clocks moved, and yet the distinction between one hour and the next, rather than insisting on the limits of numerical sequence, hung on a sign, often longer than was considered decent. There was the hour of the horse, for example: a black horse harnessed to a black carriage, stationed under the portico of the archbishop's palace, from which two priests occasionally emerged abruptly. It was affecting, almost nauseating to view this scene in the rain, and he thought this was probably owing to the acrid smell of wet priest. 'In any case, *quod videtur in imagine sacramentum est*,' he said to himself, hurriedly setting about making a series of exorcizing gestures.

Other hours were reassuring, however, if not actually consoling. The hour of the curtains was one, the hour when, although it was still afternoon, the curtains behind the windows of houses were coloured with a tender light, rather rosy or golden, because the lamps inside were already lit to counteract the murkiness of the rainy light outside. Then his glance would run along the façades of the houses, beyond which he knew there was here a clandestine brothel, there a good family with two marriageable daughters. He imagined the other light inside the houses, no more strong or clear, but more coloured and dry, in which the girls and the women patiently waited for the day to end, perhaps reading *La mort des amants* or *L'invitation au voyage*, deeply in thrall under the dictates of the day, to the worn, yellowing pages of *Les fleurs du mal*. But there were also wild hours out of doors – hours when the rain stopped and dense and obscure shapes raced across the sky, in a great hurry to get by, clutching on to one another, sometimes passing or hesitating with a motion suddenly cumbersome and slow, but always governed by the same force, sliding face down from one side of the horizon to the other. In the smoky light the immense leaden vault of the sky was in motion, borne by a silent wind that never touched the earth until, since time was also passing more slowly, it was almost a surprise when sunset came. Sunset was perhaps the pleasantest hour of the day. Sometimes an unlooked-for glance, a glare of light, one might call it, came off the sea at the level of the horizon; some façade would glitter, some window be lit up for an instant like a beacon. And immediately the cover of clouds closed over, visibly more dark, but this time more for protection than menace.

You'll catch your death of cold, his mother had said in tones of distress. Yes, you will! Why don't you take your umbrella?

I don't know, he had replied. The truth is, I don't go walking in the rain out of love of rain, but for the sake of a girl.

A girl? his mother asked, settling herself in her chair. What girl?

He began to explain that the young woman whom she

did not know was from a family in modest circumstances, if not poor; her parents would have been happy if he, the only son of landed parents, would propose. But he never declared himself either to the family or to the young woman.

I can hardly believe this! his mother had murmured, almost to herself, resting her chin on her hands to observe him more comfortably.

The truth is that up to that time my ideas about everything had been confused – except about timber – he said to himself, turning on his right side. The body, for example. What is the body? Incapable of finding a satisfactory answer through intuition, he spent entire nights in obsessive enquiry, although at that time impeded by sleep. The subject of the body had originated with this girl, whom he had seen on different occasions, fleetingly and especially from the back. She could never have seen herself from behind; looking at her, he was conscious of her vital organs – of another life, distinct from his own. Her existence was clearer and more visible, but more difficult and mysterious to imagine, the closer he felt it to his own. Certainly it was not precise to say 'closer'; rather one could say 'tending to approach'; while the simile wasn't right, it made instead a distinction and a difference: something separate from himself, which he wanted to have in his immediate vicinity, or rather within reach. Now he felt he needed to be vigilant about what she was, which she of necessity had been brought to ignore and neglect.

From these premisses, confused as they may have been, the discussion of 'body' ran, attempt after attempt, all night long, complicating itself along the way with spurious assertions. So sometimes he saw her delicate shoulders and almost imagined 'the body'; slender, and with a face whose features were unclear to him behind a curtain of hair, in the posture of reading Baudelaire; at other moments, instead, this 'body' (pink evanescent nudity) smouldered in the confusion of his weary mind, until he supplemented it with borrowed details or more pronounced curves: in fact the excessive curves of a really big girl, whom he often saw selling chickens in the market.

Immediately he rejected this mixture, indignant; but in spite of his opposition the image he had composed began again to take on its own outlines, starting at the base of the spine, let's say, progressing automatically out of the nocturnal insomnia, until the confusion of dawn appeared beyond the windows. On the terrace and in the garden the wind was domesticated, playing household games with dry gravel and blowing chairs over. The clouds ran high and indifferent towards the darkest seas, while ruffled pigeons inspected their sectors of terrain.

On sunny days, however, whether it was winter or summer, he ran to the port even before dawn. There the storehouses were already open; not the shops, but huge black warehouses piled with bales of goods, open and deserted, with a tiny oscillating light at the back. The harbour water was black and viscid, littered with shiny bits of straw. Although the air was already impregnated with light, the stars were still out in the pale sky; the mountains seemed to come closer with a leap at every blink of the eye, with denser shadows in the growing light.

Passing from night to day, the world came closer to him: with each leap it became more visible and more clear. But, he thought, this process of clearing was not perfect or conclusive: it wasn't a true clarity, but the periphery or the backcloth of clarity, the visible – the foothills of distant mountains or, from close up, minutiae of objects of different dimensions – proclaimed the reversibility of this same process. Yes, the air was transparent; yet, he said, shaking his head, there was still too much unknown.

'Too much unknown!' he repeated, turning over on his left side. The large window was now filled with a milky light. Perhaps, he thought, there is less fog.

He got up at three in the afternoon. As soon as he looked at the clock, he hauled himself out of bed. 'I must hurry!' he said. But suddenly he remembered she was not in Venice. Ah! he decided, sitting again on the edge of the bed, I may as well be calm. He was by nature, he admitted, lazy. And he suddenly felt that the world, at least from his point of view, was deserving only of his laziness.

Aside from your mother, she had asked, and your fiancée in Skipton . . .

The woman who aspired to be my mother-in-law . . . he interrupted her, laughing.

Well? Who else? she had insisted.

No one, he had admitted with a shrug. No one ever expected anything of me. Let's say that, aside from the timber, no one has ever taken me very seriously. Basically, he concluded, it has been easy for me. Easy, I suppose, as it is for an actor to perform to an empty house.

She seemed irritated. What does that have to do with

Rialto

it? Are you an actor?

He excused himself. It's only a bad metaphor. I meant that it's nice to know that no one is interested in watching what we are doing. . . .

She protested: it was foolish to think one was invisible or irrelevant. And she said other things in the same tone, sometimes raising her voice.

Why are you intimidating me? he asked her brusquely.

She looked at him amazed. No, she said, continuing to watch him, that is not at all what I meant to do!

He smiled at her, nodding. He believed her, he had replied.

Since then their conversations had become more mannered, more cautious, strewn with unexpected silences to avoid *in extremis* imaginary pitfalls. It's not true! he continued to shout inside himself with almost theatrical desperation. He would have liked to take her hands and plead with her to believe him, even on bended knee. But he was too large compared with her, too awkward: even in his imagination the scene of pleading on bended knee didn't come off. And then, apart from the pleading, what should he or could he have had her believe?

It is better to forget! he decided. By the time she returned they would both have done everything they could to forget. It would have begun all over again instead, from the beginning, with a meeting in the café or dinner at that restaurant. . . . And then, who knows, they might have found another café, another restaurant.

Suddenly the fog outside the window began to evaporate and to clear. As the vapour spread and scattered, the impertinent, rosy-veiled and almost-in-mourning image of a sun appeared, so far away it seemed to have emerged from the mists of memory rather than out of the fog.

A bad omen! he said to himself, looking worriedly at the apparition and sketching out several forms of exorcism. Suddenly he realized that this waiting of his and telling himself stories now about her return was, like the smile she had worn when they said goodbye at the station, a way of consoling himself. Certainly he wanted her to return, but the desire, to draw Plutarch's distinction, was in him, the impulse that rolls round and turns backward, not the force that drives forward.

In the bevelled edge of the mirror now there appeared an alternative image of the distant sun: no longer the usual lighted and radiant ball, but a blurry violet and blue light.

Two doorways

Epilogue

Now two months had passed since her departure and spring warmth was slowly changing into the stench of summer. The city was becoming more crowded every day and he had abandoned the Piazza and the centre of town, spending his time in solitary corners, more unassuming restaurants, another café or even tavern on the edge of a secondary canal, remote and usually silent, that still preserved something of the severity of winter in its shadows.

Naturally, however, he hadn't ceased to stop by 'their' café on the Piazza every afternoon at four, nor to move past 'their' restaurant at dinner time, but these places were now crowded with people and seemed alien to him. The waiters were either new or pretended not to recognize him; so he paid his visits in a hurry, like an obligation, which when discharged left him at liberty, that is, resigned to chance, to the banal surprise that was still concealed in the most ordinary events. His liberty was gossipy: liberty to view the minutiae from close up, in the hope of some irregularity: a lame pigeon, a cloud shaped like a pear, a dead tree. So the day, long as it might have been, had a variety of distractions which, without interrupting the monotony, lent a certain marginal distinction. There is more rubbish today! he invariably said to himself, looking around, without, however, managing to see a trace of any.

The days, becoming longer, got muddled. Perhaps that was a more apt description. But fortunately there were the nights, undoubtedly more cool and restful than the days. Often, leaning against a wall in the more deserted spots, he lifted his face to the sky, observing the interminable movement of the stars, until some cramp in his shoulder or neck forced him to move on. There was in the positions held by the stars, for all their fixity, a sense of inexhaustible depth, which included infinite displacement. And this infinity, perceptible and almost visible, reassured him. Instead of the usual phrase about pissing dogs, a fragment then came to his mind that induced calm and repose: *nox est perpetua una dormienda* – a fragment which for him conveyed the sense of an immutable truth better than any grammatical example.

Then the moonlit nights arrived like a festive repetition of the past. 'The glory of the moon!' he said, contemplating with open mouth the stream of light flooding the city, happy in his astonishment. The great impartial light with implacable cosmic determination assaulted the most garish electrical installations, turning them pale. But it was above all in the windows of small shops that this game of futile electrical vibrations and severely candid ethereality took on an intimate, domestic, abstracted tone.

It was a benign game with no winners that he observed with impartial equanimity, at length, before the window of the slightly old-fashioned hat shop in the narrowest part of the *vicolo*, while often, at a respectful distance, a cat waited, with a paw raised out of impatience, for him to move on.

Sometimes it happened that a group of people unexpectedly materialized from some corner not far away, with a clatter of footsteps or clamour of voices. Then, without waiting for them to appear, both he and the cat fled towards the wide Frezzeria and the Piazza, the cat leaping ahead of him and vanishing, perhaps in the centre of that great void in the uncontested and dazzling dominion of the moon. Certainly here by the shop all was peaceful: even the thin shadows of the passers-by, intimidated by the great light, went off, rustling discreetly because everything seemed alien and still; the benevolent intimacy of the moon playing on the windows was lost.

'Why run away?' he asked the cat. 'Let them be the ones to get out of the way.'

From that time both confined themselves to keeping close to the base of the buildings and the windows, waiting for the intruders, almost always wrapped in their indistinguishable shadows, to pass by them in single file. The shop window was certainly a modest one, but just because it was modest it was generous with its surprising effects. In fact, while a sheet of good quality glass can be assumed not to vary in width more than a light wave of medium length, so that transparency and reflection are not disturbed by visual distortions, there must have been some distortions or gross bubbles in that window, to judge by the unexpected effects: suddenly from an entire line of invisible passers-by, one peeled off its shadow briefly to reveal a part of its physiognomy, a long slender nose or a short, squashed one, the majolica clarity of the eyes, or even larger fragments; those haphazard amplifications, or some other rhetorical game of the window, then suddenly leaped in a single bound from the visible to the invisible.

It was through one of these pranks of the reflections in the window that he saw her again one evening. It was just an instant, probably as brief as the blinking of an eye, but his marvellous glass multiplied the phenomenon, repeating it and adding an unexpected detail to it at every instant. Perhaps because his memory was in play together with the reflection, this glimpse, which in reality could not have lasted more than a fraction of a second, was prolonged to such an extent that when he turned to investigate its origin, there was no one there. He could hear faint footsteps going off in an indeterminate direction. The cat too had vanished.

'Well, now,' he said, 'it's over!' Nothing lasts long enough, he thought. There had only been time to glance before the apparition vanished and all that remained was a question as to what he had seen, the thought that he might have been mistaken. For example: had she seemed beautiful to him? he asked. Dashingly beautiful! he replied. And the phrase made the modifier seem more important than the adjective; there was such a sense of speed, of abandon, even of heedlessness, that her very beauty seemed faded and strained.

'Let's think about something else!' he said. She had rushed off somewhere and he was somewhere else, rushing in search of other thoughts. Thoughts of dogs pissing on trees or even, like Actaeon, of dogs, thoughts of divine things. However, now he was rushing slowly, so slowly in fact that the hours seemed to stand still; or, rather, he was thinking so slowly that a certain image had fallen, out of weariness; and so as not leave the picture empty, another arose to take its place.

Then these disappeared and visions followed, more than any kind of mental plan, the ground-plan of his movements about the city. There were the kind of thoughts suitable for the café and the restaurant, thoughts suitable for the bridge, for a fork in the road, and for a three-prong fork in the road (coarse and vulgar thoughts, these) and above all, thoughts suitable for bed; and since the settings were often superimposed one on another as though they were transparent, no matter how trivial some of his thoughts, they were present along with his thoughts for bed. It seemed that the room and the bed in it had become more familiar to him than any other place in the city, and he used it as a habitual subject for thought.

And moreover, when he returned there even briefly in the course of the afternoon or evening, he would ask himself: What have I reached?, almost meaning, perhaps, the geometric point at which he stood in the ground-plan of the room determined according to its distance from his bed, but also a point of analogy, again in relation to the big bed, this time understood as a place of repose which he placed ideally at the centre of his existence. In any case, the hour of bed was the most firmly fixed of all the unvarying hours that made up his day, the hour in which even the rustle of time ceased and which extended beyond its own boundaries, underneath other hours that seemed to be floating there, like Venice in the lagoon.

The truth is that, whatever the hour, he always felt it was time to sleep: time had not abdicated in favour of place as at first, naïvely, he had thought it would; rather, detaching itself from the parade rhythm of clocks, it had become inseparable from things, from the room, and the bed. But there were other hours as well: hours of greeting, of parting, even of farewell: his mother at the kitchen table with her head resting on her arms. She is going away, he thought. She is going to die. He approached, and was about to touch her when she raised her head to look at him: 'Oh, the boy who sees visions in the grotto! Let's hear what he has to say: what is there in the world that you can be certain about?'

'The cat pisses on the mat?' he said timidly.

'And what if it doesn't?' she replied.

Fortunately, he told himself, this thing about pissing on the mat is common knowledge. And then, apart from cats, there are an enormous number of creatures that piss, so one could at least agree that urination is among the most easily defined of all actions. To visualize the phenomenon more clearly, one could choose a larger animal as an example: a cow, let's say, as in the phrase: the cow pisses on the field. Now, I am saying, how can one equivocate with such an immediately descriptive expression?

With the window open, the view – roof-tops, lagoon, and distant strip of land – looked weightless in the moon-light, almost as if it were about to cast anchor and drift off like Laputa. This, he thought, should summon sleep.

But to return to the subject of cows: now he could imagine an entire herd of them and even count them one by one, as one counts sheep when wanting to go to sleep. So, stretched out on his bed with the aid of a little Librium (or even more than a little), he watched the figure of a cow now gazing on him wide-eyed, pupils glassy and at the same time clouded; suddenly it jumped to one side with jerky bucking movements and sank down in the field, lying on its side. It was trembling as it tried to get up, its forelegs extended and braced, while its left buttock was still on the grass; the other cows in the herd, horrified, made a wide circle around it. Probably, he thought, it is suffering a seizure from a lack of magnesium, and could die in a quarter of an hour. Poor creature! Why not give it some magnesium, rather than waiting for it to piss to serve the footling needs of linguistic clarity?

Finally leaving the poor creature in peace, his imagination returns to the kitchen, near the table on which his mother is resting her head, and he watches her for a few minutes, remembering how he felt as a child, especially at mealtime; that he wanted to run up to her and hold on to her and her clothes, without letting go of his piece of bread with jam. That was another time, those days! he babbled now, to justify himself. His mother smiles condescendingly and that other time immediately returns: the garden, the wrought-iron chairs, leaves, wistaria blossoms and dead butterflies on the marble table in the pergola. Forgotten from the previous evening, still fastened to the pergola, the brass lantern sways with every puff of wind. Even at the height of summer it was always shady there, a transparent,

97

cool shade, stirred by the wind, because the pergola was shielded from the morning sun by the house and by the lime trees in the afternoon. On the kitchen steps the cat watches the lime trees rustle and arches its back.

What year was that? he asks himself. His mother shrugs her shoulders with indifference and the year summoned to meet the tyranny of calendars fogs over and erases itself as he watches.

She will return, he thinks. Sometimes the years fall quickly into confusion, crowding up against one another in a disorderly way; at other times, from the farthest horizon, a single year returns by itself, trotting easily, peacefully, in the open air and therefore clearly visible, but it is not always a good year, there are often years dark with regrets and remorse and distress: ugly houses, damp rooms, ailing trees, tedious lovers, times of grey socks and striped ties. The months, the days, even the hours return: March, for example; she went to the country to celebrate her dog's birthday, which is March the 25th. But now a single hour returned to his mind most clearly of all: a beautiful midafternoon, cloudy but not yet raining; an hour central to the day, but deserted, when trains depart on lesser lines. Later, though sitting on a bench with the dog between them (a sort of black setter with drool perpetually falling from its gaping mouth, leaning too familiarly against his shoulder, trying to shove him as far as possible away from her), he had known instinctively that the hour was repeatable, that it could almost retrace its steps with the same absent-minded air of desolation, all but identical, though in some different month or year to come. Perhaps the only thing left to do was wait, he had thought. And yet only now, on the brink of sleep, his waiting seemed to him to have made a great leap forward, so that what he could see no longer began or ended in the narrow channel of his own point of view.

Moonlight continued to flood the city with tireless force, casting its reflection not only on his own window but on innumerable other windows facing west; below this light, the sea stretched darkly shadowed beyond the boundaries of sight, west of the same moon, so that everything appeared to belong to the same set of currents of repeated comings and goings, strung upon the same interminable thread of time. Everything was contained in time, now *lento*, slow and wide turning, now *andante vivace*, walking at a lively pace or skipping; now there was music, perhaps from small muted flutes, a strict, but unending song of the triumph of time.

Under the spell of sleep, spreading over the silence of people and things, the story of their lives and their meetings tirelessly repeated itself; but for the first time there was no need for a subject, even a fictitious one; sleep and time, light and shade, closely interwoven, kept every event, incident or detail, every speech, sound or person in the firm embrace of their circular grammar, without giving precedence to anything: all shone with the same lunar splendour; and beyond, as well, in the deepest darkness, west of the moon, stretched the great sameness, infinitely welcoming.

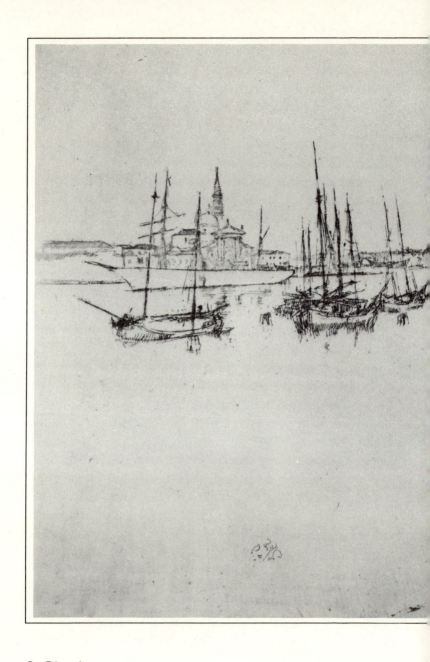

S. Giorgio